Light and Darkness

Jenna Black

Contents

1

----

2 3 1/2 years ago

"Look at her Alison, our own little darkness" Richard Swift gleamed happily as he held his newborn daughter. His wife Alison smiled weakly from just giving birth, "She's gorgeous" she said as she nit her dry pale lip, "Does this mean she'll have your powers?"

Richard quickly turned his head to her, "Of course" then mumbled "Dummy" as he rolled his eyes. "She'll inherit my ability to manipulate darkness" He put the baby down in her hospital crib just as a pair of cops barged in the hospital room. Alison gasped as she grabbed her daughter, holding her close to her chest, "Freeze Shade! You're under arrest!

Richard laughed as he opened a dark portal and blew a kiss to his wife and newborn as he jump through. Alison knew where he went as she saw a quick black figure go behind the second cop acting as his shadow.

Soon they left and Alison sighed as she looked down at her daughter, "I'll protect you"

Present Day

Jeta Smith was walking into the alley heading to the Joker's Club "Smile". She opened the door and one of his goons let her pass. She saw her best friend drinking at the bar, "Hiya Jetsy!"

She rolled her eyes at her bubbly friend, "Hi Harley, how ya been?" She spoke in her Brooklyn accent as she went behind the bar to work. "Eh, same old thing. Tryna get puddin' to stop worrying 'bout old Batsy"

Jeta laugh as she made herself a Bloody Mary, "Like that will happen, but keep dreaming babe"

After a long shift, Jeta went home after Joker and Harley left to go on "date night". She entered her run down apartment and plop down on the couch, watching the Midnight News.

"High speed chase in pursuit between Batman and villains The Joker and Harley Quinn"

Jeta smiled at this, and wished she had join their fun. Soon her eyelids began to droop covering her brown eyes.

BOOM!BOOM!BOOM!

Jeta groaned as she woke up to open the door. "Where is she?!" Joker lightly pushed her out of the way letting himself enter. "Well good morning to you too, J. Where's who?"

"Harley! She's gone, after our little fun I left her and hasn't seen her since"

Jeta rolled her eyes at his explanation, "Well idiot she's probably at Arkham, if ya left her behind with Batman", Joker got in her face and growled "Why so serious, dollface?"

A few hours later, Jeta couldn't believe that she was going to break into Arkham. J & Harley owes me BIG time for this! She thought as she transformed into a shadow sliding under the gates and her way through

Arkham. She slid against the walls like a snake through the halls carefully listening for any keys coming.

When she reached close of enough to wear Harley's personal cell she transformed back into a human. She cracked her neck and back as she walked towards the cell. She popped her black bubblegum when she noticed Harley wasn't even in there, she growled sightly, mad as hell.

Where the fuck is she?!

"Freeze!!"

Jeta gasped as she noticed at least 10 guards surrounding her, "Put your hands up Black Shadow and don't move sweet thing" One of them said as he stepped forward. Jeta giggled, "Hiya boys! Did ya miss me? Oh hey Greg" She waved to a familiar guard.

Surprisingly he waved back.

"Before ya arrest me babe, I gotta tell you something"

"What?"

"Catch me if ya can!" With that she opened a portal under her feet and fell through. It opened up as she fell through noticing it took her to the main hall, Jeta ran out the hall heading to the door.

When she was tackled by the same guard that spoke earlier. Shit! She groaned as two guards held her arms and one punched her knocking her into a peaceful sleep.

2

- -

The Next Morning

Jeta woke up in a cell to see a blurry version of someone on the ceiling of the cell twirling. She groaned as she rubbed her eyes, her vision becoming clear, "Harley?"

Harley got down and giggled, "Morning Betsy! Glad to see you're finally up", "Where the fuck are we?" Jeta asked sitting up from her bed looking around.

"We're in Belle Reve. I guess they got that tired of us in Arhkam huh?" She laughed.

Jeta looked down at her orange prison jumpsuit, Yuck I hate orange, I prefer black, She thought in her head.

"Harls, how come we're literally in a cell box? No regular block or class walls just cells" Jeta asked watching Harley go back to doing her gymnastics.

As Harley flipped and twisted laughing carefree she replied, "So I could do all of this. I kinda miss gymnastics Jet"

Jeta raised an eyebrow, "You have your own gymnastics room at home, don't you?"

Harley smirked, "Yeah sure, Mistah J got me a gymnastics room" Jeta quickly caught on and acted like she was going to throw up. A guard walked in and pointed at Jeta, "You have a visitor, let's go"

A visitor already?

The guard opened the cell cuffing her hands leading her to the visiting room. When they entered the room, the guard remove her cuffs then to turn around to see a familiar face meditating in the air.

The guard went to a corner as Jeta walked closer to her cousin, "Hi Raven". Raven open one eye to see it was her and stop meditating to sit at a table in front of Jeta.

"Jeta, why are you here?"

"All I know is I went to break Harley out of Arkham, next thing I knew I was knocked out and here I am in Belle Reve" She said somewhat proudly smiling, "What brings you here, my dear favorite cousin?"

Raven scoffed at her, "I'm your only cousin, and I'm here cause your friend Harley called me. You better be careful in here, its not like Arkham"

"Who runs this place?"

"Amanda Waller, she's a bitch but I got to admit she's a real clever one. Forget her right now, Jeta what happened to you?"

Jeta cut her eyes at her Raven, "Huh?"

"You used to be good. Now you've changed, what the hell happened?" Raven sighed shaking her head, which made Jeta chuckle a little.

"You know damn well what happened, so don't try to act confuse" She growled, twiching her left eye.

12 Years Ago

"Jeta Jade Smith, where the hell have you been?!" Her drunken and high on cocaine mother yelled at a young 12 year old Jeta throwing a beer bottle missing her head by a few inches.

"I told you I went over to my friend Harleen's place to work on our math project" She sighed rolling her eyes going down the hall to her room. "Don't you roll your eyes and walk away from me young lady!"

Alison charged after her daughter yanking her hair making her fall to her knees. Then started punching her face repeatedly as Jeta's body shook with anger. She felt her mother pick her up by her shirt collar and threw her into the hallway closet door, her spine hitting the golden doorknob.

Her ribs and stomach in pain from the constant punches and kicks.

Hell, what ever happened to "I'll protect you"? Jeta thought.

As the abuse continued, all Jeta could do was laugh, quietly at first then it got louder. Once Alison heard, the abuse stop, "What's so funny huh? I wanna laugh too"

Jeta's brown eyes turned completely black as she looked into her mother's eyes, noticing the fear. "Now ya scared, aren't ya?"

She turned into a shadow, and quickly grabbed her mother's chin snapping it, popping her neck out of place. Young Jeta laughed even harder then before as her mom was laying in a puddle of blood. The laughter changed into sobs as she transformed back to a human.

"I don't need anyone's protection anymore!" She sobbed.

"Oh come on! That shouldn't be the cause of your actions though, Jeta. It didn't have to turn you to the bad side. Stop acting like you're alone in this world cause you're not!" Raven said crossing her arms.

Jeta giggled, "Oh! I should be the one to stop acting like I'm alone in this world? At least I'm not the one publicly sulking walking around hiding my face all day and night! At least I laugh sometimes, you don't even do that!"

"You don't know me Raven! Once you realize how lonely you are in this big ass fucked up world, it changes your view on life, it depresses you and to most people it might not be good to see the world like that. When in all truth, that's exactly how the world should be view!"

With that said, the two cousins were silent, just crossing their arms not looking at each other until Raven got up from the table, walking. "I'll see you at the next family reunion, cousin" Jeta said not looking back at Raven. Once the door closed, the guard in the room cuffed Jeta again leading her out the room.

Nice to have the support I never had, She thought as she walked back to her shared cell with tears of a mixture of anger and sadness threatening to fall.

She wouldn't dare let that happen even if there was a gun pointed at her head with someone forcing her to cry or else. She would rather die then to shed any kind of tear.

3

T he Next Day

Harley and Jeta was being walked to the cafeteria, once they got there their cuffs were gone and they were free to do whatever.

They got on the lunch line, noticing the inch lady was the same one at Arkham. "Hiya, Rachel!" They both said, as Rachel smiled at them nodding. They knew she couldn't talk, since her tongue was cut off by someone at Arkham.

They were served chilli with some water to drink and a small piece of bread. That found an empty table and sat down sitting in front of each other.

"So, you still haven't told me how your visit went?" Harley said after drinking some water.

"Let's just say it wasn't so fun, Harley" As she ate her chilli, she noticed a man with body full of tattoos sitting alone eating his lunch. He looked like mystery and she just had to uncover it.

"I'll be back babes" Jeta said to Harley as she walked slowly up to his table. "Hi, I'm Black Shadow" She fake smiled holding out her hand. The man looked at her with a mix of confusion and a "Get the hell out of my face" look but he nodded at her in response then shook her hand quickly.

Jeta sat in front of him not caring if he wanted her too or not, "I like your tats, dude. They're pretty cool, I can tell they tell some kind of story"

Chato sipped his bottled water then chuckled, "Um, yeah some of em do"

"What's ya name?" Jeta asked smiling, "Diablo" He said smiling back. "You're Mexican?"

He nodded, "Well how do you feel about Trump?"

Diablo laughed, "If they let me kill him without being charged I would do it in 00.2 seconds"

Jeta joined in on the laughter. After spending the rest of lunch with each other, it was time to go.

As she was being handcuffed again, Harley stood next to her, "Did ya have fun, Jetsy?" Jeta giggles and nodded, "Loads of it. I think I like that guy he's pretty cool"

"Who was he?" Harley asked as they walk down the long halls with two guards behind them. "El Diablo or I guess just Diablo"

"El Diablo?! I heard he had a little tantrum a while ago in here and burnt the whole courtyard!"

"You're right lady, he did do that. He's a metahuman with Pyrokinesis" One the guards said to them.

So he has fire powers, Jeta thought. "Fire & shadows don't go well together Jetsy, so don't get any ideas cause he's hot" Harley laughed hysterically, "Get it, hot!"

Later on that day

Jeta was taking a nap but was half awake when she heard a creaking door open and the sound of heels walking.

She opened her eyes to see a woman on the floor above the cage walking slowly. She noticed Harley standing watching her too.

"Are you the devil?" Harley spoke watching the woman's every move. She chuckled and replied "Maybe" then walked out the door.

"Well that was creepy, and not the fun kind either" Jeta yawned, "Well I'm going back to take my nap"

The next day after that creepy encounter, Jeta and Harley were woken up by their infamous guard Captain Griggs and strapped down in chairs with wheels.

Jeta doesn't know who she hates more for abusing her best friend, Griggs or Joker. Probably Griggs since it was done right in front of her.

"Ay, Griggs were we going? I didn't sign up for no field trip!" Jeta yelled trying to move her head to see where Griggs was hut couldn't because of her head gear.

They were in the medical center, Harley went first. "Who are you? I don't know you? Who are you?! AHH!" They injected something into her neck and rolled her away.

Jeta didn't even flinch or yelp when they injected whatever the hell is was in her neck. I've been through worse pain, she thought as they rolled her away behind Harley.

They led outside and Griggs had slipped something into Harleys hand without anyone except Jeta noticing.

"You're so screwed" Harley said to him laughing. His eyes nearly popped out of his head as a different guard held him back from going any further, "W-what do you mean? Harley! Harley!"

Soon, the girls were let free and they stood up stretching, "Hi boys!" Harley smiled.

Jeta looked around noticing others around them, Killer Croc, Deadshot and Diablo. Jeta waved at him and he waved back.

Two others came, Slipknot and Captain Boomerang beating up a couple of officers in the process.

Harley spoke up, "What was that? I should kill everyone and escape?" Jeta noticed everyone watching Harley but she didn't pay her any mind, since she knew who she was talking to.

"Oops, sorry. The voices" Harley giggled pointing to her head, "I'm kidding, jeez! That's not what they really said" She smirked as Jeta laughed.

"Listen up!" Jeta looked in front of her to see Rick Flag yelling at them. "In your necks, you know that injection you got, well it's a nanite explosive. It may be the size of a rice grain, but trust me it's powerful as a hand grenade"

"So, you disobey me, you die! You try to escape, you die! If you otherwise irritate or vex me, and then guess what? You die!"

"What a nice pep talk" Jeta whispered to Harley, then Harley rose her hand. "Well, I'm known to be quite vexing. I'm just forewarning ya"

"Lady shut up!" Rick yelled at her, looking annoyed already. Harley pouted as she folded her arms and mumbled "Meanie".

"Now this is the deal..." Rick said, "You're going somewhere very bad to do something that might get you killed. But until that happens, you're my problem"

4

Deadshot spoke up, "Was that like a pep talk?" Rick stared at him, "Yeah, that was a pep talk. Now there's your shit, so grab what you need for a fight. We're wheels up in 10"

"You know you might wanna work onyour team motivation thing. Ya ever heard of Phil Jackson? Triangle bitch" Jeta heard Deadshot continued as she went through her stuff. She found some clothes and makeup, so she got dress.

"Hey Harls, look! My favorite choker" Jeta happily said as she put her blood choker and posed to show Harley her look.

"Lookin' hot babe. Shit if I wasn't straight I would totally date you" Harley laughed, "Too bad I'm already in love"

Jeta shook her head at her friend's comment then found some eyeliner, and put it on her.

"Lookin' good there mamí" Jeta turned around and saw Diablo smirking as he put on his varsity jacket making Jeta wink at him.

Soon, it was time to go in the helicopter. Jeta sat in the middle of Harley and Diablo. Her eyes started drooping after awhile, until some girl with a mask jumped inside the helicopter.

"You're late" Rick said looking at her. This is Katana. She's got my back.She can cut all of you in halfwith one sword stroke. Just like mowing the lawn. So, I would advise not getting killed by her cause her sword traps the souls of its victims"

Harley grinned and reach her hand out to her leaning across Deadshot, "Harley Quinn, nice to meet ya. Love ya perfume. What is that? The stench of death?

Katana stared at her and pulled her sword out, "Should I kill them?" Rick looked at her, "Easy cowgirl, it ain't that kind of mission. Have a seat"

After that, Jeta fell asleep. The next thing she knew she was being slapped by Harley and looked around seeing the it was now night time, the helicopter was destroyed and she was laying on the ground.

"What happened?", "We got hit by something Jet" Harley said as she help Jeta off the floor, "Shit, you really do sleep through anything"

Jeta laughed and nodded, "I guess I do"

Half Hour Later

Jeta was sick of this bullshit "Suicide Squad" mission, been fighting mutants left and right and she was so tired of fighting. Turns out all of this was to just save Amanda Waller's ass.

They all walked out to the rooftop of the building they were in, when one of helicopters appeared and began shooting at them. Jeta screamed and duck behind an air vent next to Harley and Deadshot.

"The hell is going on?!" She yelled randomly as Harley checked the phone Griggs gave her, Harley looked at Deadshot had saw the message and shook his head at her. Harley got up smiling, grabbing Jeta's hand walking to the chopper.

"Harley, no! Don't!" Deadshot yelled, as Jeta looked at Harley "The fuck is going on?"

"We're going home, Jetsy" As they got closer she saw Joker smiling staring at Harley. He drop a rope for them to grab, Harley went towards when she noticed Jeta not following her.

"The chip, what about the chip?" Jeta bit her lip, Harley didn't care about any chip since she knew hers was disarmed and she jumped for the rope catching it.

"Harley!" Jeta yelled at her best friend, "Deadshot, kill that woman now!" She heard Waller yell at the hitman who never misses.

"She ain't do shit to me, man"

"You're a hitman. right? I got a contract. Kill Harley Quinn. Do it your freedom and your kid"

Deadshot smirked, "Now she dead" walking over to an air vent, Jeta gasped "No! Don't do it"

He shot, and Harley's body went limp, Jeta ran to the edge watching it seem the world had stop moving, When will my nightmare end? She thought.

Until Harley giggled looking at Jeta waving, making Jeta smile.

"I missed" Deadshot shrugged walking pass Waller and Captain Boomerang whispered to him "Good one, mate"

"It's Waller. Savior one- zero's been hijaked. Shoot it down!"

Jeta turned quickly to Waller then saw the chopped her only best friend was in go down in shock and mostly anger. "Target destroyed, maam", "Thank you. Now get me off this roof. The Joker and Harley Quinn are no more"

"You bitch!" Jeta charged after her grabbing her neck, choking her. "You killed my best friend!!"

She felt all the boys of the squad try to get her off of Waller but she was too strong.

"Let her go! Or I'll push the button" Rick threaten her, Jeta looked in Waller's eyes it was filled with fear. She let her go and walked off the roof, feeling a panic attack coming.

As she walked pass Boomerang he touvhed her shoulder before she brush him off saying, "You couldnt save her". Jeta ran down the stairs to the elevator pressing the button rapidly.

"Open up, come on, come on! Hurry up!" She banged on the elevator. "Jeta!" She looked and saw Diablo coming towards her as the doors open. She went in and pressed the close button as fast as she could. Finally it closed, just Diablo reached it. She could hear him banging on it as she sat in the corner and screamed as shadows appear all over the closed box she was in.

"Its all your fault"

"You could've save her"

"You killed Harley

"Killed your mother"

"NOW YOU DIE FOR YOUR SINS!"

Jeta screamed as she rocked back & forth hiding in her knees. She growled as she stood up and looked at herself in the mirror in front of you. She ran to it and banged her head on it, smashing it to million of pieces.

"Do it, Jeta!!"

"Do it for your sins!!"

She picked up a piece of glass letting it make lines against her pale skin, opening blood as the shadows laughing.

"I did it for my sins" She whispered, falling into a peaceful sleep that's been waiting her whole life for.

"Here I come mommy"

The last thing she heard was "Please, stop I need you mamí!" Then everything went black.

5

Diablo heard the screams from inside the elevator, he tried to open it with his fingers. He got so fed with it he just burned the metal down.

He saw the shadows on the walls laughing, he look in the corner and saw Jeta bleeding. "Shit!" He bent down and slap her cheeks trying to wake her up. "Mí amor, wake up!......Come on wake up!" He felt her pulse, it was still there.

"Leave her be!"

"Let her rot in hell!"

"Its a wonderful place to be!"

Diablo growled and yelled for the shadows to shut up. He burned them in the process and picked Jeta up bridal style and walked towards the stairs.

"Mmm"

Jeta woke up and saw him, "Hi Chato". He look down at her, "How'd you know my real name?"

"The shadows" She smiled, her eyes in a daze. Chato reached the lobby where everyone else was, one of Rick's officers gave him a first aid kit. He cleaned and wrapped her cuts.

The squad came over, "How ya feeling, mate?" Boomerang ask. Jeta just smiled and giggled, walking out the building with everyone else.

Just as they turn the corner, looks who there. Harley Quinn, drenched in rain sitting on a cop car. Jeta stopped in her tracks as Deadshot and Chato walked up to her. Killer Croc looked at her, "You don't look so happy. Your friend isnt dead"

Jeta gulped, she was so pissed, How dare she play with my feelings?! She thought. "She played my feelings, Croc. I hate that" With that she kept walking. She heard Deashot talking to Rick.

"So let me guess, we're going to the swirling wing of trash in the sky" Rick stay silent. Swirling wing of crash in the sky, what the hell is that? Jeta thought. "You know, cause why wouldnt we? So, when does this end, Flag?"

Rick replied dodging the question, "Load up. We're in for a fight" Deadshot growled, "No! You tell everybody everything, or me and you are gonna go right now!"

At this point everyone even Jeta was watching as they walked to the "swirling wing of trash in the sky", Rick sighed, "Three days ago, a non-human entity appeared in the subway station. So Waller sent me and a woman with incredibles abilities, Enchantress, a witch. See, nobody could get near this thing, but the witch could"

One of his soldiers interrupted, "Bombs ready, sir" Rick turn to him "Set for two seconds. You just press the button and drop it" Then turn to the group, Um, needless to say the whole thing was a bad idea and she bolted. Thats how she escaped from Waller. So, now you know"

Everyone didn't express any feelings as they look at each other. Deadshot spoke up "Look, you can just kill me, but I'm going to have a drink" He started walking to the bar and everyone followed, even Katana.

"Hey! Deadshot, I need your help" Rick pleaded, making Deadshot chuckle, "No, sir. You need a miracle"

Harley got behind the bar, "What you guys in the mood for?"

"Beer", Croc said as she sat on the leather sofa. "Whiskey", Katana said Deashot already made his drink, Harley looked at Chato "What about you hot stuff?"

Chato looked up, "Water" Harley giggled, "That's a good idea hun" She turn to Jeta "And you, Jetsy?"

Jeta didnt answer her just got up and grabbed a bottle of hennsey then sat next to Chato. Harley noticed the tension she was giving her and didn't say anything about it. Once everyone had what they want Deadshot decided to make a toast.

"Heres to honor among thieves" Katana interrupted, "I'm not a thief" and she walked away.

"Oh, she's not a thief. Well, we almost pulled it off. Despite what everybody thought. The worst part of it is, they're gonna blame us for the whole thing, they cant have people knowing the truth. We're the patsies, the cover-up. Don't forget, were the bad guys"

Everyone drank their drinks, in Jeta case she gulped down half of her bottle. Chato spoke up, "For about two sweet seconds...I had hope" Deadshot raised an eyebrow, "You had hope huh?"

Chato nodded turning his stool towards him, "Hope dont stop the wheel,from turning, my brother"

"You preaching now?" Diablo continued, "Its coming back around for you. How many people you killed, man?" Deadshot shook his head, "You dont ask nobodyno question like that, ese"

Chato stared at him, "You aint ever whacked down no women. No kids?" Deadshot stared back, "Nah, I dont kill women and children"

Chato sighed, "I do. See, I was born with the Devils gift. I kept it hidden most of my life, but the older I got, the stronger I got. So I started using it for business, you know. The more power on the street I got, the more firepower I got"

"Like that shit went hand in hand, you know? One was feeding the other. Ain't nobody tell me no. Except my old lady, she used to pray for me, even when I didnt want it. It was like God didn't give me this, so why should he take it away?"

His voice started cracking, "See when I get mad, I lose control you know, I just...I dont know what I do...till its done" Jeta felt for him, she rubbed his back, he didn't mean to kill his wife, he was born with something he didn't know how to control. Just like her.

Boomerang spoke up sadly, "And the kids?" Diablo didn't answer as the tears fell from his eyes"

Harley gasped, "He killed them. Didn't you?!" She growled, "Own that shit.Own it! I mean come on, what'd you think was gonna happen? Huh?"

Jeta stood up, "Harley shut up!"

"No! She yelled back, "Let's lay it all on the table, Miss Black Shadow! You killed ya mother! You killed -"

"Shut up Harley!"

"You killed an airplane full of people! Flight 202 in 1998! Hundreds of people lost their sons, daughters, uncles, aunts! All cause of you! Ya even killed your sibling!"

Jeta was furious, she laughed louder....And louder....And louder....Till her vision went black

6

"Swing low, sweet chariot,Coming for to carry me home.Swing low, sweet chariot,Coming for to carry me home.I looked over Jordan, what do I see,Coming for to carry me home.A band of angels coming after me,Coming for to carry me home"

Eight year old Jeta watched her mother sing in her old rocking chair, watching her mother knit a pink sweater.

"M...Mama? Wilma's crying"

Alison smiled gently at her oldest daughter, "Go feed her for me, can't ya see mama's busy"

Jeta walked into the room she shared with her 5 year old sister and picked her up, "What do you wanna eat?"

"No hungry" Little Wilma smiled, "Want Jet". Jeta giggled and went outside to the backyard to play with her sister.

They played in the driveway, laughing and giggling. Nothing could wrong.

"Let's go in mama's car and drive like her"

"Ok" Jeta smiled.

Jeta heard the shadows telling her to attack Harley, but instead Jeta kept laughing, "Now that's funny Harley. Who told you that story? Raven?"

She grinned even creepy than the Joker, who knew that was even possible. She took her half empty bottle of liquor and walked to the bathroom as Harley began her rant again, "What you were Diablo just....Thinking you can have a happy family....Coach little leagues and make car payments? Normal is a setting on the dryer. People like us, we dont get normal!"

Boomerang gave Harley a disgusted look, "You may be pretty amazing on the outside, but deep down you're ugly"

Harley rolled her eyes at him, "We all are! Except for him" She said pointing to Croc. "He's ugly on the outside, too" Croc scoffed as he took off his hoodie, "Not me, shorty. Im beautiful" Harley smiled at his confidence, "Yeah, you are".

At this point Chato went to check on Jeta, he walked inside the women's rest room. "Jeta?....It's me bonita, Chato" He saw all open stalls until he got the sixth one and knock on it.

"Please go away" Jeta's voice sounding broken and tired. "I can't do that mamí, so come out" Chato pleaded. "Don't make me crawl under there"

Jeta came out the stall, eyes redder than someone smoking weed. Chato caressed her cheek, "Don't listen to Harley"

"I...I should have told her no" Chato assume she was talking about sister, "We shouldn't have drove the car, it was my fault crashing into that tree"

"Mi amor, shh. It wasn't your fault. Your friend in there was just being bitchy" He said hugging her tight, kissing her forehead.

Jeta could smell his cologne, as she hide her face in chest listening to him. "It wasn't your fault in your case either. You didn't know how to control it, plus you can't change what you did"

Chato bit his lip and pulled away from the hug. "Ya know mi amor, I really like you, You're like a sexy sombra to me". Jeta giggled, "A sexy shadow huh? Never heard of that one before"

"I see you know Spanish" He smirk, "Que yo puedo hacer gritar papi en la cama" He grab her ass firmly and kissed her, not even letting her a chance to kiss back then left the bathroom, Oh shit, she thought, I think I need new underwear. She bit her lip and followed him out. When they walked back in the bar and sat back into their seats, well Jeta's seat was Chato's lap.

Deadshot noticed this, "Shit yall finally got together, Boomerang you owe me ten bucks", Boomerang groaned, "I got you mate when I get my wallet"

"Hold up, homie. Ya'll made a bet on us" Chato stared at them, "I made a bet too" Harley smiled at Jeta hoping that she'll forgive her. Jeta didn't smile back just gave her a blank expression.

Rick walked in and sat next to Deadshot making Harley glare at him, "We don't want you here" He ignored her turning to Deadshot. "Ya get to the part in that binder saying I was sleeping with her?" He nodded, "Yeah. I never been with a witch before"

Rich shook his head in shame, "The only woman I ever cared about is trapped inside that monster. If I don't stop the witch, its over. Everything is over.....Everything". He pulled out a huge stack of letters, "You're free to go. By the way your daughter writes you everyday. Literally, every single day" He started walking away.

Deadshot took the stack and caught up to him grabbing his shoulder, "You had these the whole time? You had letters from my daughter the whole time? Fine, I'm gonna get you there And you're gonna end this. I'm gonna carry your ass if I have to, cause this shit is gonna be like a chapter in the Bible. Everybody's gonna know what we did, and my daughter is gonna know that her daddy is not a piece of shit".

Boomerang and Jeta follow them out the door, "Hey! I'm coming too" Harley got her bat and started walking when she noticed Croc and Chato watching her, "What? You got something better to do. Come on!....Pussi es"

7

7

As they reached their destination, Deashot asked Chato if he was gonna fight with them. Chato hesitated, "What if I lose control?", "Shit, then maybe well have a chance" Deadshot smiled.

"Hey, everyone can seeall this trippy magic stuff right?" Harley asked. "Yeah why?" Deafshot replied raising an eyebrow. "I'm off my meds", "Me too Harls" Jeta smiled making Harley hug her tight.

"Oh god, Harley you know I don't like hugging people" She giggled but hugs her back anyway. "I'm sorry, Jetsy" Harley whispers in her ear with tears in her eyes.

Jea rubbed her back, "Its ok, but next time that happens I might kill ya" Harley smiled wider, "Deal and happy birthday"

Jeta nodded as they pulled away, "Thats your old lady huh?" Deadshot look at Rick, "Yeah". "Well, you need to handle this shit, all right? Get up there, smack on her ass, and tell her knock this shit off"

Jeta spoke up, "I don't think that's safe"

"I've been waiting for you all night. Step out of the shadows, I won't bite. Why are you here? Because the soldier led you and all for Waller?" The witch laugh, "Why do you serve those who cage you? I am your ally and I know what you want. Exactly what you want"

"Jeta, baby girl. Time to get up"

Jeta woke up in her bed back at her mother's.

"Good morning sweetie", "Happy birthday Jetsy" Her parents said.....Her parents?

Both of them?

Her father, the same one who was sentenced to 20 years in Arkham and has only seen her during visits? No fucking way.

He took her hand and pulled her out the bed, "Wakey, wakey. Go in the kitchen we have surprise for you"

Jeta went into the kitchen, and saw her sister, a birthday cake and a pink banner getting her a happy birthday.

"Hey Jeta, happy birthday" Wilma said hugging her.

Wilma look just like her but with her mothers hair color and fathers eyes. The doorbell rang and Wilma told her to it's a surprise for her. Jeta open the door and saw Chato. "Happy birthday babe" He grabbed her hips and kissed her passionately. First time in her life, Jeta's happy, she's got everything she wants.

"Wake up!"

"It's not real, mamí. Wake up"

Jeta woke up, It was all a dream. She sighed, thinking about her family but bit her lip thinking of that kiss.

Chato rubbed her shoulders, proud that he got her out of her trance then move to the others. Deadshot, Harley and Rick were in a trance too.

"It's not real" Chato said. Deadshot looked out of it coming out of his trance, "I killed the Bat" Chato shook his head, "Nah homie, you dont want that"

Harley scoffed as she came out of her trance, "What? I want that", Chato rolled his eyes, "She's trying to play games with you man. It's not real!" Rick came out of his dream, "He's right. It's not real"

As the group walked up to the witch, she stared at Chato, "How long have you been able to see?" Chsto smirks, "My whole life. You can't have them" He says pointing to the squad, "hese are my people right here, especially her, my lady" He looked at Jeta then back to the witch.

Hmm, maybe part of the dream is becoming a reality

8

The witch smirk at Chato, "Brother, make them bow to me" Her "brother", Incubus popped up out of no where, Jets thought he looked like a bunch of wires put together, "Oh wow! We should run"

Everyone hid being something. "GQ, come in. We're in position" Rick said into his walkie talkie, then mumbled, "e gotta get him in that corner, that's where the bomb will be" Chato cleared his throat, "I'll do it! I'll get him there!"

"Are you loco?" Jeta glared, Chato shrugged, "I already lost one family. I ain't gonna lose one another" Rick shook his head, "Think this through"

Chato stood up, I got this. Let me show you what I really am" He ran over to the Incubus, blasting him with fire, "Over here!"

Jeta feared he would get hurt and tried to get up to help but Harley stopped her.

"Get him to the corner Diablo!"

Chato was fighting him with everything he had. It wasn't enough until he turned into fire. "Diablo, drive him into the corner!" Rick yelled

"Get him mate" Boomerang whispered. "Come on", "Yeah, do it!" The others yelled.

Once he was in the corner with the Incubus, getting strangled by him. Rick yelled again, "Diablo, get clear! Get out of there!", Chato turned to him, "Blow it!" Deadshot sadly looked at Rick, Blow it" Rick gulped and spoke into his walkie talkie, "Now GQ, now"

Jeta eyes almost popped out of her head, "NO! Rick what the hell?!"

"Everybody down!"

While everyone fell down, Jeta didn't. She turned into her fullest, most dangerous form, Black Shadow and ran towards Chato. She grabbed Chato out of his hold and kick Incubus down towards the bomb as it went off.

After what seemed like ten hours of sleeping, Chato woke up seeing his Deadshot and Rick looking down at him. "Hey ese, glad to see ya alive" Deadshot dais as he and Rick helped him up. "What happened?"

He turned to see Harley crying, holding Jeta and his heart broke.

9

"No, no, no, no!" Chato rushed over to her, Harley snapping at him, "Don't get any closer you idiot! Why didn't you move from the bomb?!" She yelled tears running rapidly down her face as she push him away from her best friend.

Chato hated himself for what he did, he didn't know what to say to Harley. "It's not his fault, doll face. She made the choice to do it." Deadshot said patting Chato on the back.

"Well, if he did move, she wouldn't have done it right?" Oh boy, if looks could kill.

"Enough! Of all who have faced me....you have earned mercy. For the last time, join me....or die" Enchantress spoke watching everyone.

Harley stood up, looking at Deadshot, "I'm not much of a joiner, but maybe we should" She shrugged making the hitman's eyes pop out, "Hey! She's trying to take over the world"

Harley scoffed, "So? What's the world ever done for us anyway? It hates us!" She walked up to the witch, coveung her eyes from her light.

"Hey lady? I lost my Puddin' and my best friend over there. But you can get em back, right?" Harley said with a tone of hope.

The witch smirk with delight, "I can, my dear. Anything you want"

"You promise?"

"Yes child. You need only bow and serve beneath my feet" Harley smiled, "I like what youre sellin' lady. Theres only one teeny problem" She said ad she slowly got down yo pick up a sword.

"You messed with my friends!" She yelled as she stab the witch, and grabbed her heart. "Her hearts out!" Yelled Rick.

Meanwhile in a corner, Chato was holding Jeta, kissing her face. "Wake up, mamí please, I'm sorry" He begged, tears about to fall down.

"Chato" a voice faintly said. "Oh great, I'm hearing shit now" Chato groaned rubbing his face.

Jeta sighed, moving his hands quickly kissing him making Chato pull away in shock. Jeta giggled at his face, "I'm not that easy to kill. I'm too beautiful to die, but too wild to live"

Chato hugged her tightly, feeling like never letting go until he heard Rick yelling to witch. They watch as he broke the heart, crying as he walked away.

Jeta got up, "Your lady isn't dead, Flag" Everyone looked shock to see her alive, "Geez, Flag you got two ladies?", Boomerang laughed.

"No not me, even though I'm flattered. Look" Jeta pointed to the dead witch. Something was moving, fighting to get out. A woman broke free, crying with joy.

"June!" Rick ran to her, picking her up. "I thought I killed you. I thought I killed you" Everyone smiled at the sight, at least something went right tonight. Croc sighed starting to walk away, "Y'all don't mind. I got me a sewer to crawl back into". Deadshot chuckled, "Yeah, and I got some business to handle back in Gotham"

Harley turned to him, "I'm going to hotwire a car. Need a ride?" He scoffed, "Ya crazy ass is not driving", "Oh come on, why not?" Harley pouted.

Just then Waller walked in holding up her badge making me growl, How the hell is this bitch not dead yet? Jeta thought. "Come on Waller, we just save the world" Jeta stared at her, making Harley nod. "Yeah! We just saved the world. A "thank you" would be nice"

Waller rolled her eyes and mumbled, "Thank you". Jeta smiled, "You're welcome. So, we did all this shit for no reason huh?"

"You get ten years off of your prison sentence"

Deadshot shook his head, "Nah, that's not enough. I'm seeing my daughter" He stepped up to her, Waller sighed, "Fine, that can be arranged. Any other requests?"

Harley raised her hand, "An expresso machine"

"BET" Croc said.

Jeta moved forward, "Freedom. I did nothing wrong to get sent here anyway"

Waller chuckled, "You snuck into Arkham Aslyum". "Ok, so what? No one died or got hurt. I didn't steal anything. Now let me go free!" Jeta growled getting into her face, Chato trying to hold her back.

"Fine"

Jeta looked back at Chato, "Let him free too"

10

J eta sat on the couch in the famous Teen Titans tower, she had to "move in" for awhile since she got evicted. Its been a week since she was let free.

"Hey Jeta", she looked up seeing the hoy wonder. She wanted to laugh cause men in tights crack her up, but for once she didn't. "Hello Robin"

"Um, Raven said she'll be back soon to take you house hunting", Jeta nodded in response, "Cool bird boy". Robin gritted his teeth, "My name's Boy Wonder - I...I mean Robin! Urgh!" He walked out the living room in a hurry, making Jeta laugh.

Honestly, Jeta didn't feel like house hunting. She was feeling depress, didn't have any clue why. She took out her black diary and began to write;

Lost

The darkness surrounds meIt's getting so coldI'm all aloneWith no one to hold

My world is so emptyAll what's left is painNo sunshine to light my wayJust never ending rain

I drown in tearsMy heart is cryingNo one seems to noticeMy soul is dying

She turned a page and wrote again;

Something Lost

I had it once, now it's goneLike a knot it's been undoneWas once so tight, now so slackHappy times I wish I could have backI sit a home, and feel so lonelyIt'll be great if that was all, if only...Zombie on the outside, the living deadBut so many questions floating around my headConfusions rains down, it poursPandora's Box, I've opened the doorsNo sign of anyone who can helpNo sense of feelings or of myselfWhere I can find the answersWho am I? What am I? Am I a dream? Or am I the dreamer? Am I a thought? Or a complex computer, How do my thoughts start? What makes them end?What makes me do this? What makes me do that?I know I overanalyze, I can't help itThinking and gazing into space, as I sitWhy can't I accept the wisdom of those aroundNot letting myself accept the answers I've foundI want to free myself from my mindAnd not just to pretendEverything's okay everything's fineI want to be NORMAL....When it's going to end....

"Jeta!"

Jeta jumped and shut her diary. It was Raven entering the room, "Let's get this over with". She got up and went inside the elevator with Raven, she noticed watching her. "You ok?"

She look back at her and smiled, "Perfectly fine" Raven didn't question her anymorex taking her word for it. Actually believing her cousin was fine. In Jeta's mine she couldn't believe it herself, Guess she doesn't know by now when I say I'm fine, I really mean no I'm not, please help me.

An hour later, Jeta picked out a house. It had big backyard that led to the woods, five bedrooms, six bathrooms, nice kitchen with a dining room, a game room, huge living room, and a pool. It also had Jeta's favorite thing a library.

"You really like this place, huh Jet? Are you happy" Jeta genuinely gave Raven a smile and a nod, "Yeah". I'm happy for now, it'll end soon, She thought.

"I gotta talk to you Jet"

"We're already talking" Jeta said as she lean against the wall.

"The Teen Titans - Well, I need a favor. We want you to join our team. It'll be fun, you and I fighting crime like we used when we were younger. Since I bought you this house, I was hoping it would be your present in joining us"

Jeta stared at her for a good 15 seconds, then giggled. "Really? That's why you got this house for me. Not even to just help out a family member? Just to help out yourself"

Raven pointed her finger in Jeta's face, "You need to clean up your act! Stop acting like this!" Jets shook her head, "I'm fine on my own. By the way, here's some advice, don't point your fucking finger in crazy people face!"

This time it was Raven's turn to shake her head. "You're not crazy, just stupid and worthless"

"What you gonna do for furniture? You don't have any money" Raven went on rolling her eyes, hoping Jeta wouldn't ask her to buy any, since she bought the house.

Jeta smirk catching Raven's attitude. She snap her fingers and a big portal appear. Soon, the whole house and backyard was decorated and furnished.

"You just stole this shit!" Raven growled, making it Jeta's turn to role her eyes. "You ain't gonna buy me this shit. So shut up and get out my house"

"You can't kick me out, I brought this place!" Raven fold her arms stepping forward. Jeta laughed, "Ya name ain't on the lease though. So bye Felicia!"

Raven glared at her and zapped herself to wherever. Jeta giggled at how much she could piss her cousin off as she walked to the library.

You're just stupid and worthless

The words were playing over and over in her head as she walkes in the library and sat on the couch.

Its not my fault. Its not my fault. She kept thinking, soon she started saying it out loud whispering, "Its not my fault, its not my fault.... It is my fault"

Water fell from her eyes rapidly. She couldn't control it this time. Her breathing fasten as she cried, holding her knees up to her chest.

"Its my fault"

Sources for poems;

Source: http://www.familyfriendpoems.com/poem/lost-a-dying-soul

Source: http://www.familyfriendpoems.com/poem/depression-and-anx iety

11

J eta walked into Waller's office, the woman at her desk with a file of papers watching Jeta sit in front of her. "What's up, Waller?"

Waller smirk, handing her a picture, "Do you know this man?"

She gulp as she answers, "The man whose pull out game is weak". Waller surprisingly chuckled, "Yeah. Your father, right? The Shade. Well, I know where he is"

Jeta folded her arms as she stared at the photo, still listening to Waller. "He was seen and captured last night, after trying to rob a bank. He's here now at Belle Reve"

"Would you like to see him?"

Of course I do, Jeta thought. "I'll think about it, is that all?"

"No" Waller replied picking her walkie talkie up, "Bring him in"

Jeta eyes widen hoping it wasn't her father, she turned around and saw Chato which made her smile. "He's free to go now". Jeta jump into his arms, making him smile as he caught her.

"Let's go home, bonita" He whisper in her ear before kissing it. He starts to walk away, still holding Jeta until Waller interrupted. "Don't forget you're both still on my watch. Don't do anything dumb because this time your sentence will go as order"

In all honesty, Jeta wasn't even paying attention to her warning. She was just happy to be with Chato.

An hour later, Jeta was cooking Mac and cheese, and tacos for Chato. While she cooking, she was dancing and singing loudly.

"Do you remember the time, when we fell in love? Do you remember the time, when we first met? Do you remember the time, when we fell in love? Do you remember the time?"

She was dancing like they did in the video mastering it perfectly. Chato stood in the doorway watching trying not to laugh. For a good two minutes Jeta didn't notice him until she turn around.

"How much did you see?" She giggled, Chato messed her hair up, "All of it. You even got the moves like in the music video down"

Jeta glared at him, "It's a short film!"

Sorry its short.How do you think Jeta feels about her dad?Vote & comment

12

"**J**eta"

"Jeta"

I open my eyes to see darkness, "Who's calling me?"

"You don't remember your dear father" The shadow chuckled. "What the hell is this?" I growl, noticing I was in my shawdow form. "What's happening?"

"I'm haunting your dreams, sweet child. I missed you, my dear" My father said walking to me...well floating since he was in his shadow form too. I scoff at him.

"You didn't miss me. You've been gone all this time. Why come back?!"

"To love you"

"Get out of my head!"

"I'll be back Jeta Smith, I'm your father"

"NO! LEAVE ME ALONE"

"LEAVE ME ALONE!" I jumped up awake now out of bed. I put my knees up tovhest as I notice Chato stirring. He groan as he sat up looking at me, "Que esta pasando?"

I shook my head as he rubbed my thigh, "I'm fine baby. Just a bad dream". His face show concern, "Wanna talk 'bout it?"

I shook my head again and he nodded as we both laid back down. He put his arm around me and laid his head against my back falling back asleep. I look in the mirror on the ceiling. I look at myself and i hat what i see. It's been now four months now that I've been with Chato, its been the best four months honestly that I've had.

Last week, I found out I was two weeks pregnant, so I'm pretty happy about that. I haven't told anyone about it, not even Chato. Only thing that was messing me up even more than I'm already am was my father. I still haven't seen him in jail, I wanted too but I don't.

Chato and I still work for Waller, we still do missions with the Squad. Harley's back with us, she got herself caught and sent back to Belle Reve, I believe on purpose.

A ringing sound broke me out of my thoughts. It was Chato's phone since he was knocked out I picked it up.

"Hello, this is Chato's girlfriend. Who are you and why are you calling at 5AM?"

The person chuckled, "Its Flag, Waller wants you guys to come in right now. Says its a surprise for Chato. You got an hour to get here" With that said he hung up.

I put the phone back and shook Chato awake. "We gotta meet Waller. She got something for you" He rolled his eyes as he got up. We got there in an hour when we walked in her office there were two figures sitting in each chair. They didn't look back at us, Waller cleared her throat.

"Morning, Diablo. About five weeks, the jail has received two new inmates. A brother and his sister"

"Ok where's she going with this? Why would he care?" I thought.

"Since then I found out they were metas and I've been testing them" She said proudly and as coldly as ever. "Turn around kids"

They turned around, my eyes widen. They look like Chato. I turn to him and saw he started crying as the little kids hugged him crying too while calling him daddy.

He bent down to their level buying them tight repeating that he was sorry.

"Hate to interrupt this reunion but you two got a mission to go on" Waller snapped her fingers and two gaurds walked up to the kids. They started crying harder, "Please no! Waller give me twenty minutes with them please" He begged.

She sighed and nodded, "Take your father to your cell, guards make sure they do"

One guard was in front of us and the other in the back while we walked to their cell. Once we got there, it was tiny very tiny. The kids sat on one bed while Chato and I sat on the other.

"Daddy who is she?" They stared at me,making me nervous. "She's my girlfriend. Jeta these are my kids. The ones I thought I accidentally killed, Bella and Julien"

Boy if looks could kill, I would be dead for sure.

13

W ow! Over 600 reads & over 40 votes, glad you guys like it so much□ Keep reading cause there's soooo much more on the way & I know its too late to say this, hut happy Thanksgiving___________________

"Great, just met not even 10 minutes ago and I'm already hated", I shook my head ignoring their stares, until a cute kinda squeaky voice spoke, "You're pretty, more than my mommy" I looked at Bella and smiled.

I could tell she took more after her mother. She smiled back at me, holding her pink teddy bear as Julien didn't pay me any attention.

"How did you guys end up here?" Chato asked, "That lady Waller found us at an orphanage. One day, the lady in charge caught us using our power. I guess she called her or they knew each other" Julien said.

A guard open the cell door and speaking of the devil. She walked in pointed at Chato and I. "Let's go now, Flag's waiting"

"Wait!" Bella stood up, "Can we go too?" Waller and Chato said no as she pouted. Soon Waller gave in allowing the kids to come. I left Chato to help them pack and went to the courtyard.

"Hey look who it is, Lil' Miss Jet" Deadshot chuckled, wrapping his arm around me. I waved to the gang, Croc patted my head and Bommerang pinched my cheeks.

"Why harass me so much?" I chuckled, "Oh hush, you're like a baby sister to us, mate" Boomerang said before drinking his beer. Flag came around and looked at the group, "Where's Diablo?"

I pointed behind him, he turn seeing Chato coming holding Belle and Julian by his side. "What the hell? Diablo who are they?"

"Hey mate, they kinda look like ya. Ha! What, they your kid or something?" Boomerang laughed before taking another sip of beer. Chato smirked, "Yeah they're mine"

Boomerang choked on his beer. "I thought they...you know" Croc said, making me giggle a bit, "We thought so too. Guess we were wrong huh?"

Flag sighed, not really wanting to watch over kids but didn't say anything. After the rest of us got our weapons we got on the chopper. Of course, Katana was late just like last time. It honestly felt weird without hearing Harley's jokes and giggles. I hope this mission doesn't involve her in anyway.

After about an hour of flying, it was dark out and we landed on a road. "Finally a smooth landing" I joked as Chato helped me off the chopper. I heard a few other giggles from some of Rick's men. We started walking behind Rick like last time.

This place look so familiar to me, I don't know where we are but it looks .....comforting to me.

"Yo, Flag!" I yelled making him look back at me then kept walking. "Where are we?" I ask walking next to him. He didn't look at me, "You'll find out soon" I stop in my tracks watching everyone go by me.

"What's wrong, baby?" I felt Chato hold my hand. I shook my head, "Nothing, papí" We all were following Flag. The place was like Gotham, but more run down, like a Gotham hood you could say. The place was quiet....too quiet. It was dark too, like really dark. We all had flashlights to see.

I saw something dark flash by from the corner of my eye. A cat shadow, but no actual cat in sight.

"Look out!"

I fell to the ground, feeling something on me.

"Hello again Jeta, welcome home"

Oh shit

14

I kick the shadow off of me, and it groaned as it hit the ground. Chato and Croc help me up as the figure stood up, "Well geez, Jet. That's how you treat an old friend huh?" It transformed into a human, my friend Anabelle. She rubbed her burgundy ombre hair as her brown eyes smiled at me.

I squealed and hug her tightly. "I haven't seen you in forever!", "I know, last time I saw you, we were 12"

"Ana, where are we?", I don't what I said but it made her laugh, really hard. "You don't remember this place?" She ask and I shook my head. She sighed, "Of course you don't. This is home, our home, Shadesville"

Shadesville. Village of shadows. My parents...well my mom and I used to live here till I was 12. Everyone was either a shadow or a human during the day or night. Wait a minute, why are we here?

"Flag? Why are we here?" He didn't answer me, just shrugged. Damn liar. I turn back to my childhood friend, "How's everyone else?"

"We're all still the same. Darren's still Darren, funny and crazy as ever. Willow is still smart, and has a crush on Dex. Hex is still herself, and Dex is still gay"

I chuckled, thinking about my memories with the "Midnight Assassins" That's what the neighborhood called us, we were always causing trouble somewhere without a care in the world. I look back at The Squad, "This is my squad, we're the Suicide Squad. There's Killer Croc, Deadshot, Captain Boomerang, Katana, Rick Flag, and El Diablo my boyfriend and his two kids"

Ana nodded in acknowledgment, then held my hand, "Let's go visit the crew" I look at Flag for approval, "Go ahead, this is a long mission anyway might be here for a few days. We'll find a hotel"

Ana motioned her finger for Chato and the kids to come with us, "Y'all can stay at our place. We got room for ya" I looked at her in shock. "You still have the house?"

"What, you think we would sell it or some shit? Must be out of your mind....Hell, then again you always were" I smiled as she walked up in front of us now. I walked with Chato, "So this is where you used to live huh?"

I nodded, "Yeah, kinda sad I didn't remember it at first"

(A/N; If you know this house, I fuck with you)

After a five minute walk, we entered the run down house, it still look the same with the "Beware" sign out on the lawn. "Yo! Guess who's home?!" Ana yelled.

The fraternal twins Hex and Dex were in the living room and rushed to the front door. Their green eyes widened and they both hug me tight, tighter than Ana did. "Jet!!", "What's up Hex and Dex?"

The jet black hair, feckled face boy pulled away put his hands on his hips, "The hell you've been, Missy? Couldn't wrote or call none of us"

"Yeah" His sister agreed giggling, "Couldn't tell us you were married, had kids and shit!"

I felt myself blush as Chato look at me smirking, "Um, we're not married yet and these aren't her kids" He said gently. The twins looked at each other and each pulled out a $20 bill and gave it to Ana.

She thank them as they walked back into the living room, "Why did they give it that?" Chato ask. "We all made a bet that she wouldn't be married with kids by the time she was 23"

I shook my head, "That's so sweet of y'all". She laughed as she headed up the stairs, "Come on, see your rooms" Ana showed the kids their room, then showed Chato and I room.

We heard the front door close and hear a deep voice yell out that they were home. I smiled knowing that voice, it was Darren.

Ana notice my smile and leaned over the railing, "Dar! Come up here got a surprise for ya" I heard his footsteps getting closer then he walked in.

"Hey Darren, I'm back"

He didn't say anything just picked me up, whole spinning. "Welcome back Jet" He put me down then I introduce him to Chato and the kids.

"Alright D, let's leave em alone to rest" With that Ana and Darren left the room.

It feels good to be home.

How do you feel about Jeta's friends?

Do you think Flag's hiding something? If so, what?

Vote & comment

15

It was the next morning and I was walking with Hex and Willow to nowhere actually, just walking around. "So, Jet? How's Gotham" My brown skin old best friend, Willow ask. Her head was shaved because she just didn't like her hair.

"Gotham's gritty, full of criminals"

That made them giggle, "So its basically here. Just with thousands of us" She said. Hex wrapped an arm around me, "Ya know, when ya left, none of us got a chance to say goodbye to you"

"Yeah" Willow replied, "What happened? After you, ya know got arrested?"

12 Years Ago

"What happened, young lady?"

"I killed her" I simply replied, smiling proud of my actions. "She hated me, so it doesn't matter, Mister ummm..." I look at his badge, "Mr. Gordan"

He shook his head, told one of officers to put me in car. As the guy held my arm walking to the car I noticed my mom's lifeless body going into the ambulance. They had block off the roads near the area, caution tape all over. Behind the tape, I seen my crew.

They've came all the way to Gotham to see me. They looked scared at what I had done, but smiled proudly knowing I was free.

2 hours later;

I was being put in my cell in Arkham, it wasn't really big but wasn't small at all. The white walls surround me except for the clear wall in front so the guards could see me. That Gordon guy must have had someone bring some of my stuff, I saw all of my books of poetry and my diary I had just started using. I sat one the bed and heard someone laughing.

"Looky, looky. Fresh meat" I looked across the hall and I saw a creepy smile, really white skin with red lips. That's how I met the Joker & how my life changed.

"Well" I spoke up, "That's what happened, girls" They just looked at me as we were walking down the street. People stared at us....mostly at me, fear on their faces. If I could read their thoughts, "Oh shit, its Jeta", "Its that the Black Shadow".

Oh how I live for people fearing me, it brings such joy to my heart.

I was brought out of my thoughts as Hex asked, "At least we're all free now, back together again for now" I chuckled at her words, "You think we're free? You think you're free?", I scoffed and continued. "We're heathens, we're never free" They ignored me. Out of the group, Willow and Hex are probably the only changed ones, they so called have change their ways for crime. Shit, even if they did, people will still treat and see them as criminals no matter what they do.

"I'm not a heathen" Hex replied and Willow agreed which made me stop walking to laugh out loud which made all the strangers watch. "You're a fucking heathen! Don't deny your past, embrace that shit! Own it! We killed people, robbed the poor and the rich for fun"

"Shit, half of the stuff we did was either yours or Willows idea! So don't act like all innocent. If y'all wanted to be normal, you shouldn't never did the shit you did! We're the Midnight Assassins, fucking own it" I growled and a hear a buzz from the beeper Flag gave the Squad.

I didn't say goodbye to them as I stormed off going to the hotel everyone else was in.

16

- -

When I got into the hotel room, Flag told me to meet him at, everyone was in there, even the little ones. "So what's up boss?" I asked him as sat next to Chato on a bed.

"We need to kill a dangerous shadow"

"A shadow? More dangerous than me" I scoffed, "Impossible" My comment made the kids giggle. To be honest, I'm glad they're starting to accept me, I guess Chayo talked to them I guess.

"Oh, it is possible sweetheart. Now we're going to downtown"

I looked up at him, "Downtown? Flag, there is no downtown"

Everyone looked at me confused. "This is the village of shadows, demons.. ..shadow-demons. There is no such thing as a downtown, besides the grave yard"

"That's our downtown, the grave yard. Where whoever dies their soul rests there, its not good to wake up souls" I warned him. He smirked, "Well tell the dude we're after that. He's trying to wake up these souls and used them in his army"

Deadshot spoke up, "Who's he?" We all nodded since we were thinking that same thing. "Never mind who he is, just know he's dangerous. Now we leave at midnight to find him"

After the little meeting, I went back to the house. Chato and the kids stay behind at the hotel. I walked in the living room to see Darren and Ana making out. I rolled my eyes, "Shit, get a room"

They pulled away from each other, Ana smirked, "Hush like we didn't hear you and ya little lighter going at it the other night"

I scoffed, "Ain't nothing little about that man" I giggled which made Ana join in and give me a five high. "Boy in the room here" Darren growled. We ignored him and went into my room.

"Heard about your little rant" She began as she sat down the bed, "Now I'm not gonna make you apologize" I looked at her, kinda shocked. Anabelle is like the mom of all of us, always telling us to treat each other good. It's like Darren is her husband, Dex is her only son and Hex, Willow and I are her daughters.

She went on, "I agree with what you said. They've been trying to "act normal" like that's possible for them after we just robbed and blew up a bank two blocks away a few weeks ago"

"Need to suck it up and move on" I mumbled, laying on a pillow.

I could tell she was watching me as I closed my eyes. "Think of it from their point of view though, they love it but its not their passion anymore. They know they can't afford to just stop being a villain, they'll be jobless.....homeless if they quit." With that said, sh got up and left me alone with my thoughts.

I started thinking about my favorite movie, The Breakfast Club. How it reminded me so much of my own clique, how we're all different but somehow have similar issues. I guess, Allison was right, when you grow up. Your heart really does die.

Later at midnight, I was walking with the the squad to the graveyard. It was foggy and dark as usual, I wasn't scared though, I love the scent of darkness. Kroc stood next to me, "You know anything bout this graveyard, shortie?"

I nodded, "Place where dead souls, spirits go. Not just any souls though, it has to be a bad one. Basically this where they bury them but after that they go to hell"

I noticed everyone had heard me and looked a bit scared to be dealing with actually demons, Chato doesn't count since he uses his power for good. "Ay, Flag? Anything else we might need to know about this guy"

"He's a metahuman, same powers as Jeta" He quickly said. Same powers as me, what the hell?

"Enter my dears" A creepy voice said as the wind blew. We walked into the grave yard, I was holding Chato's hand, ok I'll admit it I was a little scared.

A shadow was standing on top of a tomb, smiling creepily. "So glad you come make it" That voice sounds so familiar to me.

Next thing I knew the shadow had summon two more shadows and they lifted me in the air, making me scream. "Jeta!" I heard Chato and a few other members yell out. The main shadow laugh, not even. It cackled in a cringy, evil way. Like my father did....

The show transform into a human reavling my father. "Welcome home honey" He cackled even more. That soon ended when fire was sent his way, I smiled knowing it was Chato. Deadshot and Flag tried shooting him but missed.

"Now that's not a good way for your friends to introduce themselves, Jeta" He smirked, raising his hand at all three of them, making more shadows attack them.

He threw me on the ground and hovered over me. "What ever happened to my sweet angel?" I laughed, feeling my madness take over my thoughts. "I'm playing the villian, daddy. Just like you wanted" I kick him off of me, making him land a few feet away.

"How dare you come back to ruin me even more?" I zapped him with a bolt of darkness, then swiped my finger cutting as if I was cutting him. The darkness cut him, making my motions a reality on his face. "You left us! Just acted like you forgot you had a wife and two kids"

"That you've murdered" He stuck back with darkness choking my neck. "Shit, you need me. I'm the only relative besides Raven and her father that's alive. I'm sure she doesn't treat you right anyway, so you need me"

He put a gun near my belly, "Plus I know your secret"

17

Oh shit, I thought as he held the gun to my stomach, I was scared he would pull the trigger but knew he wouldn't.

"You know how it feels to lose a love one. Bet ya don't wanna lose anymore" My father smiled. I hear Chato yell out, "What the hell is he talking about?" I glanced at him to see him getting frustrated.

My father looked at him, "Ooh!...You didn't know! My dear eldest child is pregnant" I saw Chato freeze, watching the gun and back at me. I gulped, Well I didn't want him to find out this way. "Pregnant?" I heard him say.

I managed to turn into my shadow form and choke him with a rope I found on the floor, till his face was blue. I knew hee smiling, "Gonna finally kill your old man?"

"Do it. Go ahead"

I tightened the rope more, but I let him go. For some reason, I could kill my mother and little sister...but not my evil father. "Jet! What are you doing, kill him!" I heard Flag yell at me. I look towards him with tears falling, "I-I can't. I'm done killing my own family!" I turned to face my dad, he held a gun up to me, I was stunned as Chato was running towards me. "No!"

Bang!!

He shot me.....my father really shot me.....

I woke up in a white bright room. I looked around and saw a doctor in front of my bed, I looked at her name tag, Dr.Quinzel. "Oh, good morning Ms.Swift. Glad you're awake" She said. I asked her what happened. "You're very lucky the bullet didn't hit any major organs"

"What about my baby?"

"She's fine" I smiled at the fact, that it's girl, but I had to ask, "Are you related to Harlenn Quinzel?"

I saw her smile fade as she nodded, "I'm her mother...Tell her that we miss her and still love her" Dr.Quinzel left the room.

Meanwhile

Chato was in the waiting room with his kids, waiting on the doctor to hear about his girlfriend and new baby.

"Dad? Do you miss mommy?" Max asked him. Chato turned to him and nodded, "Of course I do, Max" (A/N; Yeah I changed his son's name)

"Do you still love mommy?"

Chato gave him a blank stare then nodded. "I'll always love her, Max" Max went back to reading his Spiderman comic book. "You really do love Spiderman, don't you Max?" Chato asked remembering when Max used to have a big collection of Spiderman all over his room, comics, posters, pencils, he had it all.

"You know he's not real right?" Bella giggled.

"A boy can dream, little sister. Plus the Black Cat doesn't exist either" Max smirked. Dr.Quinzel walked up before an argument could happen.

"Mr.Santana, she's alive and rested, so is your baby. You can see her and fill out the discharge forms if you want"

Chato and the kids went into Jeta's room, where she was watching the news on the TV, Villain The Shade has been caught and arrested by the Suicide Squad. "Jet, are you okay?" Little Bella said sitting nest to Jeta. "I'm fine Bella, don't worry" She replied, kissing her forehead as Max put a get well teddy bear in her lap.

Chato leaned over and kissed her lips, "I love you Jeta"

"I love you too babe" Jeta smiled brightly for the first time in a while. A smile she actually meant to do , a smile full of love and happiness.

"You're the light to my darkness, Chato"

"Ewww!" Bella and Max giggled leaving the room.

.

.

.

.

.

.

.

.

Well that's the end of this story, it's bittersweet ending this.......Or is it?

Yeah its not the end just kidding more coming soon